Tell me Something
Happy
Before I Go to Sleep

Joyce Dunbar · Debi Gliori

DOUBLEDAY

London · New York · Toronto · Sydney · Auckland

Willa was tired,
so Willa went to bed.

She lay with her pillow this way...
...and that way...and another way.
But Willa couldn't sleep.

"Willoughby," called Willa.
"Are you there?"
"Yes," answered
Willoughby. "I'm here."
"I can't sleep," said Willa.
"Why can't you sleep?"
asked Willoughby.
"I'm afraid," said Willa.
"What are you afraid of?"
asked Willoughby.
"I'm afraid that I might
have a bad dream,"
said Willa.
"Think of something happy,
then you won't have
a bad dream,"
said Willoughby.

So Willa tried to think of something happy, but she couldn't.

"Willoughby," called Willa. "Are you still there?"

"Yes," answered Willoughby. "I'm still here."
"What can I think of that's happy?"
asked Willa.
"Oh, lots of things," said Willoughby.
"Tell me. Tell me something happy
before I go to sleep."

Willoughby thought for a moment.
Then he said,
"Willa, look under your bed."

So Willa leaned over and looked under the bed.

"What do you see?" asked Willoughby.

"I see my chicken slippers," said Willa.

"That's right," said Willoughby.

"And do you know what your chicken slippers are doing?"

"No," said Willa. "I don't."

"They are waiting, just waiting, for nobody's feet but yours."

"Good," said Willa. "That's happy. What else?"

"What do you see on the chair?" asked Willoughby.
"I see my blue and white jumpsuit," said Willa.
"Do you know what your jumpsuit is doing?"
said Willoughby.

"No," said Willa. "I don't."
"It is longing, just longing, for
tomorrow, when you will
jump out of bed to put it on."
"Good," said Willa. "That's
happy. What else?"

Willoughby picked Willa up
in his arms and padded
softly downstairs to the
kitchen. He opened the
larder door.

"What do you see on the
shelves?" asked Willoughby.
"I see bread and honey
and oats and milk and
apples," said Willa.
"That's right," said Willoughby,
"all waiting to be made
into breakfast, for you and me to
share."
"Oh good," said Willa.
"That's happy. What else?"

Willoughby carried Willa into the
sitting room and switched on the lamp.
"What do you see in the corner?"
asked Willoughby.
"I see my basket full of toys," said Willa.
"What do you think they are doing?"
asked Willoughby.
"I don't know," said Willa.
"They are dreaming, dreaming of tomorrow,
and the games you are going to play."
"That's very happy," said Willa. "What else?"

Willoughby carried Willa to the window and opened the curtains wide.

"What do you see in the darkness?" asked Willoughby.

"I see only the night," said Willa.

"What do you think the night is doing?" asked Willoughby.

"I don't know," said Willa.

"The night is waiting, waiting for the morning, which is on its way round the world."

"That's happy," said Willa.

So Willoughby carried Willa back to bed.

"What do you see in your bed?" asked Willoughby.

"I see my ted," said Willa.

"What do you think he is doing?" asked Willoughby.

"Waiting for me to snuggle up," said Willa.

"That's right," said Willoughby, "waiting especially for you."

"There's just one sad thing,"
said Willoughby.
"What's that?" asked Willa.
"The morning is waiting for you, too.
It's waiting to wake you up."
"But I'm awake already," said Willa.
"That's why it's sad," said Willoughby.
"The morning likes waking you up.
That's what makes the morning happy."

"Willoughby," said Willa.
"What is it?" said Willoughby.
"I'm tired."

*"The morning is waiting too," said Willoughby.
"What for?" said Willa.
"Oh, lots of things,"
said Willoughby.
"What things?"
asked Willa.
"For grass to grow in,
flowers to bloom in,
leaves to flutter in.
For clouds to float in,
wind to blow in,
sun to shine in.
For birds to fly in,
bees to buzz in,
ducks to quack in."*

*"That's a lot of happy
things," said Willa.*

"And when the morning
wakes me up, will you still
be here?" asked Willa.
"I'll still be here," said Willoughby.
"Good," said Willa. "That's the
happiest thing of all!"
"Goodnight Willa," said Willoughby.

But Willa didn't answer.
Willa was sound asleep.

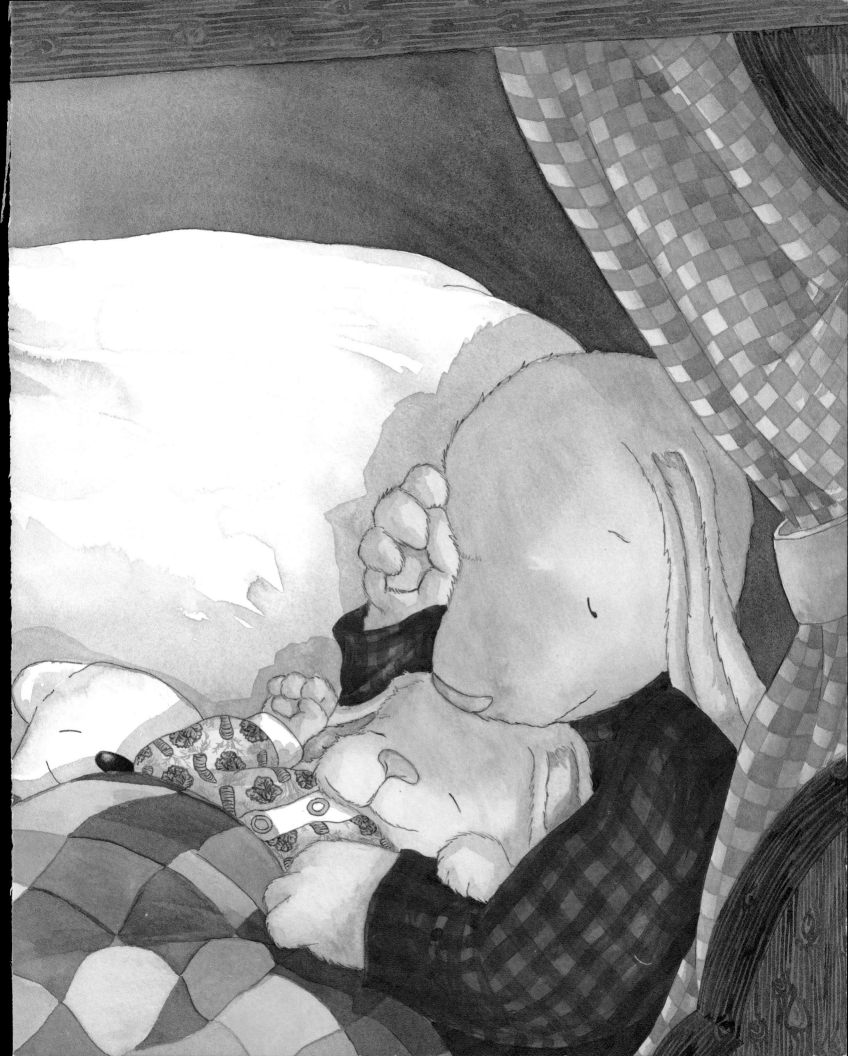